THE WOMAN WHO KILLED THE FISH

THE WOMAN
WHO KILLED THE FISH
AND OTHER STORIES FOR CHILDREN

CLARICE LISPECTOR

translated from the Portuguese by Benjamin Moser
with illustrations by Marian Bantjes

STORYBOOK ND

Published by arrangement with the Heirs of Clarice Lispector and Agencia Literaria Carmen Balcells, Barcelona. Originally titled *A mulher que matou os peixes*, *O mistério do coelho pensante*, *Quase de verdade*, and *A vida íntima de Laura*

Manufactured in the United States of America
First published clothbound by New Directions in 2022

Library of Congress Cataloging-in-Publication Data
Names: Lispector, Clarice, author. | Moser, Benjamin, translator.
Title: The woman who killed the fish & other stories for children /
Clarice Lispector ; translated by Benjamin Moser.
Other titles: Mulher que matou os peixes. English
Description: First edition. | New York : New Directions Publishing, 2020. |
Originally published in Portuguese in Rio de Janeiro by Ed. Sabiá in 1968
under title: Mulher que matou os peixes.
Identifiers: LCCN 2020012675 | ISBN 9780811229609 (hardcover) |
ISBN 9780811229944 (ebook)
Subjects: LCSH: Children's stories, Brazilian—Translations into English. |
Domestic animals—Juvenile fiction. | CYAC: Domestic animals—Fiction. |
Short stories.
Classification: LCC PZ7.1.L5695 Wo 2020 | DDC [Fic]—dc23
LC record available at https://lccn.loc.gov/2020012675

10 9 8 7 6 5 4 3 2 1

New Directions Books are published for James Laughlin
by New Directions Publishing Corporation
80 Eighth Avenue, NY 10011

CONTENTS

THE WOMAN WHO KILLED THE FISH

For Nicole and Cássio
For João, Mark and Giancarlo
For Karin, Letícia, Mônica, Zilda and Azalia
Especially for the National Children's Campaign

That woman who killed the fish unfortunately is me. But I promise you I didn't do it on purpose. Me of all people! who doesn't have the nerve to kill a living thing! I don't even always kill cockroaches.

I give you my word that I'm someone you can trust and my heart is kind: around me I never let a child or an animal suffer.

So for me of all people to kill two little red fish who weren't hurting anybody and who don't ask for much: All they really want is to live.

People want to live too, but luckily they also want to use life to do something good.

I don't yet have the nerve to tell you right now how it happened. But I promise I'll tell you by the end of this book and you, the ones who are going to read this sad story, will forgive me or not.

You must be wondering: why only at the end of the book? And I'll answer:

"Because at the beginning and in the middle I'm going to tell some stories about animals I've had, just so you can see that I only could have killed the little fish by accident."

7

I'm hoping that, by the end of the book, you'll have come to know me better and will grant me the forgiveness I'm asking for the death of two "little red guys"—at home we called the fish the "little red guys."

Beforehand I'm going to tell you a few very important things so you won't feel sad about my crime. If it were my fault, I'd own up to you, since I don't lie to boys and girls. I only lie sometimes to a certain type of grownup because there's no other way. Some grownups are so awful! Don't you think? They don't even understand a child's soul. A child is never awful.

For now all I can say is that the fish starved to death because I forgot to feed them. Afterward I'll tell you about it, but secretly, nobody but you and I will know. I hope that by the end of the book you can forgive me.

I always liked animals. I spent my childhood surrounded by cats. I had a cat who'd sometimes give birth to a litter. And I wouldn't let anyone get rid of a single one of the kittens.

As a result the house ended up being fun for me, but hellish for the grownups. At last, no longer able to stand all those cats, they secretly gave away the cat and her last litter.

And I was so unhappy that I fell sick with a high fever. Then they gave me a toy cat to play with. I wasn't interested, since I was used to living cats.

The fever only passed much later.

Anyway, let's change the subject.

Before getting started, I want you to know that my name is Clarice. And you, what are your names? Whisper your names and my heart will hear you.

I ask you to read this story all the way to the end. I'm going to tell you a few things: my house has natural animals. Natural animals are the ones we didn't invite over and didn't buy. For example, I never invited a cockroach to have a snack with me.

My house has lots of natural animals, except rats, thank God, because they scare and disgust me. Almost all mothers are afraid of rats. Not fathers: they even like them because they enjoy hunting and killing this animal that I hate. Do you feel sorry for rats? I do because they're not an animal that people can love and pet. Would you pet a rat? I bet you all aren't even scared and are a lot braver about many things than I am.

I have a friend who, when he was a boy, had a white rat as a pet. That made me so sick that I only want to take my friend's hand when the shock is over. His rat was a girl and her name was Maria de Fátima.

Maria de Fátima died in an awful little way (I say little because deep down I'm happy about it): a cat ate her as quick as we eat a sandwich.

As I was saying, the natural animals in my house weren't invited over. They showed up, just like that.

For example: I have cockroaches. And they're very ugly and very old cockroaches who aren't of any use to anyone. To the contrary, they even gnaw on my clothes in the wardrobe.

Do you know that I had a whole big war against the cockroaches and that the winner of the war was me? Here's what I did: I paid some money to a man who does nothing else in his life but: kill cockroaches. This man does something called extermination. He spreads this stuff all over the house. The stuff has a very strong smell that doesn't hurt people but makes the roaches so confused that they die.

But it seems that one roach, before dying, whispers to the other roaches that my house is dangerous for their sort, and that's how the news spreads through the roach world and they don't come back to my house. Only six months later do they work up the nerve to come back, but then I call the man with the stuff again and they flee once again.

Cockroaches are another animal I feel sorry for. Nobody likes them, and everyone wants to kill them. Sometimes a kid's father runs all over the house with a slipper in his hand, until he gets one and whacks it until it dies. I feel sorry for roaches because nobody feels like being nice to them. They're only loved by other roaches. It's not my fault: who asked them to come? They came without being invited. I only invite animals that I like. And, of course, I invite big people and small people.

You want to know something? I just made up my mind this minute to invite boys and girls to visit me at my house. I'll be so happy that I'll give every child a piece of cake, a nice drink, and a kiss on the forehead.

Another natural animal in my house is ... can you guess? Did you guess? If you didn't guess it doesn't matter, I'll tell you. The other natural animal in my house are little lizards. They're funny and they don't do any harm. Quite the opposite: they love eating flies and mosquitoes, and that's how they clean my whole house.

I don't kill lizards but some people cut them up with their slippers. And then something odd happens: each piece of the lizard starts moving all by itself. For example, a lizard's leg that's been cut off will keep moving around on the ground for a long time. It's a mystery that the pieces move around before dying.

What I also don't understand is the awful taste lizards have for mosquitoes and flies. But of course: since I'm not a lizard, I don't like the things they like, and they don't like the things I like.

Once we caught a mosquito and looked at him close up with a powerful lens. And you can't imagine what a mosquito's face looks like. It's very weird. I'm not afraid of mosquitoes or flies, but both of them bother me a lot. The lizard, who's my great friend, helps me with great pleasure because a mosquito for a lizard is almost like a dessert. We, people, like desserts with coconut, for example, but the lizard might even think a dessert like that is nasty.

Lizards don't talk, don't sing, don't dance, don't like people because they're afraid of people. Lizards would be dangerous for us if they were as big as alligators.

Now I'm going to talk about animals I've invited over, just like I've invited you all over. Sometimes an invitation isn't enough: you have to buy them.

For example, I invited two rabbits to live with us and paid some money to their owner. Rabbits have a very secret history, I mean, with lots of secrets.

I even once told the story of a rabbit in a book for little people and big people. My book about rabbits is called: "The Mystery of the Thinking Rabbit." I really like to write stories for children and grownups. It makes me happy when people big and small like what I wrote.

If you like to write or draw or dance or sing, do it because it's great: as long as we're playing around like that, we don't feel lonely, and our hearts warm up.

Getting back to rabbits, there are people who eat rabbits. I couldn't do it because it would be like eating a friend. The two rabbits we had at home were my friends.

We also had here at home two ducks we bought who spent all day following people around with that funny way they have of walking, and thinking that we were their mothers. When I meet you, I'll imitate the way ducks walk.

Another animal who thinks we're his mother is any chick. In that respect a chick is just like a person: he misses the warmth of the hen-mother. A nice thing we can do for a chick who's squawking and crying because he misses her is take him in our hand and warm up his body. When we touch them we feel their tiny heart beating inside their fluffy and warm body. Underneath the soft feathers you can feel the tiny little bones of their ribs. Chicks are always skinny. And when they're away from the hen, they can die just like that. I've bought lots of chicks and most of them died. The only ones who lived longer were the chicks with a stronger soul.

As for dogs, I've had two.

Here's what the first was like: I was living in a land called Italy. One day, walking down the streets of the city, I saw a mutt. Mutts are so smart that the one I saw immediately felt that I was nice to animals and right then and there shook all over wagging his tail.

As for me, all it took was one glance to fall in love with his face. Although he was Italian, he had a Brazilian face and the face of someone named Dilermando. I paid some money to his owner and took Dilermando home. I gave him some food right away. He looked so happy for me to be his owner that he spent the whole day looking at me and wagging his tail. I figure the other owner beat him, so Dilermando was happy to get a new owner.

Dilermando was almost as smart as a two-year-old child. He ran everywhere behind me so he wouldn't feel lonely. And he ate so much of everything that he quickly got fat.

He spent all day smelling things: dogs smell things in order to understand them; they don't reason much, they're led by the love of other people's hearts and by their own.

Dilermando liked me so much that he'd almost go crazy when he smelled with his snout my woman-mother smell and the smell of the perfume I always wear. This perfume is called in French "Vert et Blanc," which means "Green and White," and was invented by a man named Carven. As you can see, there's a little bit of everything in this world: women who beat dogs, other women who never beat them, a man who earns money killing roaches, a man who mixes some things up and invents a perfume. I'm telling you this so you'll remember when you grow up that there's a lot you can do in life.

Anyway, getting back to Dilermando's smell. He hated taking baths, he thought people were rotten when we forced him to make that sacrifice. Since it took a lot of work to bathe him every day and since he'd run out of the bathtub all covered in soap, I ended up only bathing him twice a week. The result, of course, is that he had a very strong dog smell and I immediately smelled it with my snout, because people have a snout too. Do you have a snout? I bet you do, because, besides being people, we're also animals. People are the most important animal in the world, because, besides feeling, we think and make up our minds and speak. Animals speak without words.

You know how I had to separate from Dilermando? It was because I had to leave Italy and go to a country called Switzerland. And in that country the hotels didn't let dogs in. So I chose a very nice girl to take care of him. When I was saying goodbye to him, I got so sad I cried. And Dilermando cried too.

Many years later I was living in another country that is called the United States of America. And I bought an American dog whose name was Jack. I don't remember what breed he was because I don't care, I like all human and animal breeds.

Jack was one of those big dogs who bark all the time and keep an eye on the house so no robbers can come in.

Jack only did a few things in his disciplined life: he barked, ate, flirted a lot, kept an eye on the house, slept, played with us.

He had a very exciting life because he liked everything he did. Just like me, because I do lots of things in life and I like what I do. I do a lot of things I don't like, just because I have to. Jack was less intelligent than Dilermando, but he was a very courageous dog. He wasn't afraid of anything.

You know what happened? Here's what happened: at night Jack would stay in our yard in front of our house and he thought he was such a big deal that he started watching the whole street, even though nobody asked him to. When someone, all the way down the street, would come by, he'd bark so much that he'd wake up the whole neighborhood.

Until one morning a neighbor showed up in his pajamas and said he was tired of not sleeping and that, if Jack stayed with us, he'd shoot him.

The neighbor was really angry, and I could tell he really would kill him. In order to save Jack's life, we gave him to a very nice family that lived on a farm and where Jack could bark all he wanted.

Those two happy dogs were the only ones I've ever had.

Now I'm going to tell a story about monkeys that's a little funny and a little sad.

Just imagine that I'd gone out to do some shopping and when I came back and walked in the door I felt that something weird was going on. All the people were on the back balcony and I went to see what was happening there.

Can you believe that I never expected to find what I saw there: a monkey. In fact it was a capuchin as big and strong as a young gorilla. He was quite agitated and nervous because he still didn't know the house very well. Out of pure restlessness he suddenly ran up the clothes that were hanging out to dry, dirtying all the clean clothes. From atop the clothesline he shouted like a sailor giving orders on a boat. And he was throwing banana peels that fell right on top of our heads.

Anyway, this huge capuchin monkey came to live with us. Whenever I'd go to the laundry room he'd get so excited that he'd jump from one side of the room to the other, making a mess of everything.

You all know very well that the monkey is the animal that most resembles people. This monkey even seemed to have a human life. He acted like a crazy man. Since he made a terrible mess, I decided to give him to some kids in the poor neighborhood who loved monkeys. At home everyone was sad and upset with me.

More than a year went by. One afternoon I was walking down the street in order to buy Christmas presents. The streets were packed with people buying presents. In the middle of all those people, I saw a group gathered round, I went over to see: it was a man selling several monkeys, all dressed up like people and very funny. I thought that everyone at home would love to get a little monkey for Christmas. I chose a very soft and pretty little female monkey, who was very small. She was wearing a red dress, and wearing earrings and necklaces from Bahia. She was very sweet with us, and slept all the time.

She was baptized with the name Lisete. Lisete sometimes seemed to smile begging our pardon for sleeping so much. She hardly ate, and stayed in a little corner that was just for her.

On the fifth day I started to wonder whether everything was all right with Lisete's health. Because her calm, quiet behavior wasn't normal.

On the sixth day I almost shouted when I figured it out: "Lisete's dying! Let's take her to a vet!" A vet is a doctor who just takes care of animals.

We were all very frightened because we already loved

Lisete and her little woman's face. Oh, my God, we liked Lisete so much! and we so dearly wanted her not to die! She was already part of our family. I wrapped Lisete in a napkin and we got in a taxi and hurried to an animal hospital. There they immediately gave her a shot so she wouldn't die right away. The shot was so good that she even seemed to be cured once and for all, because all of a sudden she got so happy that she ran all around the room, giving shrieks of happiness, making funny little monkey faces, crazy to please us. That's when we discovered that she really loved us and that she hadn't shown us before because she was so sick that she didn't have the strength.

But, when the effect of the shot wore off, she suddenly stopped again and sat all quiet and sad in my hand. The doctor then said something horrible: that Lisete was going to die.

That's when we understood that Lisete was already very sick when I bought her. The doctor said not to buy monkeys on the street because sometimes they're very sick. We asked very nervously:

"What now? what are you going to do, sir?"

This is what he answered:

"I'm going to try to save Lisete's life, but she has to spend the night in the hospital."

We went back home with the napkin empty and our hearts empty too. Before I went to sleep, I asked God to save Lisete.

The next day the vet called to let us know that Lisete had died in the night.

That's when I understood that God wanted to take

her. My eyes filled with tears and I didn't have the courage to tell everyone else the news. Finally I did, and everyone was very, very sad.

Since he missed her so much, one of my sons asked: "Do you think she died wearing her earrings and necklace?"

I said I was sure she had and that, even dead, she'd still be lovely.

Also because he missed her so much, my other son looked at me and said with great tenderness:

"You know, mommy, that you look a lot like Lisete?"

If you think I was offended about looking like Lisete, you're mistaken. First of all, because people really do look like little monkeys; second, because Lisete was full of grace and very pretty.

"Thank you, my son," is what I said to him and gave him a kiss on his face.

One of these days I'm going to buy a healthy little monkey. But forget Lisete? Never.

Well, now you can take a little rest because I'm going to tell a story that's so terrible that it almost sounds like a cops and robbers story. It's a story of love and hate mixed up in a single heart.

Are you rested up? Well, then listen very carefully because this story about a dog really is terrible. Don't think I'm making these stories up. I give you my word of honor that my stories aren't lies: they really happened.

Okay, get ready because I'm going to begin.

A friend of mine, named Roberto, had a dog whose name was: Bruno Barberini de Monteverdi. It's a long name for a dog, but that's what he was called. When we wanted to talk to him we just said Bruno, because otherwise his name was enormous.

Bruno had a friend, also a dog, who was keeping an eye on a neighbor's house. This dog-friend of Bruno's was named Max.

They were such good friends that they'd call out to each other, inviting each other over for lunch and sticking their two snouts into the same bowl of food. Of course neither Bruno nor Max could talk, they just barked. And their invitations to lunch at the other's house were transmitted like this: barking a little, wagging a tail, standing in front of the other one, and suddenly walking. Then one dog would understand that he was supposed to follow the other and have lunch together.

I forgot to say that Bruno Barberini de Monteverdi was madly in love with his owner, Roberto. And he was very faithful. Bruno wouldn't let anyone get too close to his owner thinking that they were going to attack him. Every night he'd wait up for his owner to come home and only went to sleep when he got back. I'm telling you this so that you can understand the tragedy that happened.

One day, Max was having lunch at Bruno's house, when Bruno's owner came into the kitchen. It's not known why Max decided to rub up against Bruno's owner. And in order to do that he came over to the owner and touched his leg.

Bruno was surprised for a second: he thought Max was going to attack Roberto and ran to defend his owner.

In order to defend his owner, he leapt on top of Max,

who hadn't done anything wrong. But Max, finding himself ferociously attacked, reacted. And the result was a bloody battle.

Max was stronger than Bruno. Bruno was being mangled. Finally, Roberto managed to separate them.

Bruno was gravely wounded and almost dying. His heart was almost no longer beating. Roberto took Bruno to the animal hospital straightaway. There they gave him a shot to get his heart beating again. They took care of the wounds on his body and on his head, and Bruno spent many days in the hospital. Until he was well and could go home.

Now I ask you: what did Bruno do? Bruno was so courageous that, once his wounds were healed, he went to attack Max.

Max then gave him the biggest thrashing you can imagine. And this time the wounds were so severe that even Bruno's ears were shredded. Roberto took him back to the hospital, where, this time, Bruno spent two months. When he was better, he went back home.

And now you tell me: what do you think Bruno did?

That's right. Bruno went to take revenge and attacked Max.

But this time he was so, so outraged that he grew stronger and turned into a devil.

And he, finally, killed Max.

Yes, but in the dog world it's different. There's no police for them to file a complaint. So dogs have to settle their arguments themselves, playing the role of judge and police, and often act like armed robbers. Dogs don't forgive each other.

What happened is that the neighborhood dogs turned against Bruno and wouldn't forgive him for Max's horrible death.

So, to get back at him, they started to stalk Bruno. Bruno by now was even afraid to go out into the street. When he'd go out, he was very leery, looking both ways.

Finally, seeing that nothing bad had happened, he started calmly going out again. And that was Bruno's big mistake.

One afternoon he was strolling along all by himself and even regretting the death of Max, who was his only friend. He really missed him. You don't find a good friend every day. Dogs have big souls, they even understand us. The world of dogs is full of love to give, and they give it without asking for anything in return. Bruno was really sad missing the friend he'd killed out of love for Roberto.

On such a sad afternoon, when he wasn't even enjoying smelling things, a dog suddenly appeared on the corner.

And suddenly on another corner another dog. And then, from the neighborhood houses, three more dogs emerged.

Bruno immediately realized that he was surrounded by several huge, strong dogs. Bruno knew that revenge is the law of dogs. He wanted to escape but couldn't break through. The dogs formed a kind of circle around Bruno.

And the circle was getting smaller and smaller. Until the dogs managed to trap him next to a tree.

The dogs then suddenly attacked Bruno all at the

same time, meting out justice themselves, because, as I said, in the world of dogs they themselves are judge and police. It was five dogs against Bruno. Bruno still tried to defend himself but was powerless against them.

And what happened was what you'd expect: the worst thing. The five dogs punished Bruno until he died.

And that's how Bruno Barberini de Monteverdi died forever and ever.

Do you miss Bruno? So do I. The story of Bruno Barberini de Monteverdi's life and death is a great love story.

Bruno loved Roberto so much that he wouldn't let any other dog rub up against him or attack him. There was also a great brotherly love that connected Bruno and Max. But his first love was Roberto.

Did that story make you sad? I'm going to ask you a favor: whenever you feel solitary, that is, lonely, find a person to talk to. Choose a grownup who is very good for children and who understands that sometimes a boy or a girl might be suffering. Sometimes just because they miss someone, like Australian parakeets. I know a girl who plays piano very nicely in theaters. This girl got an Australian parakeet for her birthday. She only got the female. The worst thing is that if you give an Australian parakeet you have to give two: a male and a female who, because of their species, are so loving that they spend the whole day kissing and can't be separated. The parakeet even fell ill because she missed her friend so much.

Well, after telling the rather sad story about the longing parakeet, I want to cheer up and cheer you all up with another story.

I'm going to talk about something very nice: an island. Would you like to have an island just for you and your friends? I'd really like that and I don't have one.

But a friend of mine bought an island just for her and her friends to relax on. You all know what an island is? it's a piece of land surrounded by water on every side.

What I'd like is for you all to come with me to visit my friend's island. You could go swimming in the sea, run after animals, and sleep in a hammock at night. You wouldn't be afraid because I'd sleep in the same room, protecting every boy and girl.

In the sea by this island there's everything: every species of fish. There are even sea horses. It's lovely to see a sea horse swim: they even look like men and women slowly dancing.

This island is a little bit enchanted.

Why? Because of the always-new air, because of the grasses called sapê that seem to sing in the wind, because of the city of butterflies. My friend and a group of her friends were exploring the island, and in the middle of a bamboo grove they found the city of butterflies. In that clearing they live, fly high, fly low, fly all around us. Little, big, blue, yellow and multicolored. It looked like a dance of butterflies in that silence that only an island has.

The silence of the island is a different silence: it's pierced by the characteristic sounds of the animal and vegetal inhabitants. Plants, if you know how to touch them, have leaves that seem to sing.

And they talk to people. What about? It depends whether you're sad or happy, hungry for beauty and for conversation.

My friend bought the island in order to let children live there for a while, the slightly sad children who hadn't yet talked to plants and animals. A sea horse greeted my friend when she was swimming in the sea.

The sea floor there is blue and of every other color, because of the sea urchins and starfish and algae that move around, giving it that swaying coloring.

You think I'm making this up?

But if I swear to God that everything I told you in this book is true, would you believe me? Then I swear to God that everything I've told you is completely true and *really happened*. I respect boys and girls and that's why I don't ever trick them.

Good, thanks for believing me. I don't like to be thought of as a liar.

Besides the schools of big and little fish, in the sea around the island there are also schools of porpoises and dolphins: they look like little whales.

The land animals are the birds of every size and color. There are also lots of snakes and lizards. The house on the island keeps its doors and windows closed because of mosquitoes, lizards, and snakes. There are also herds of tapirs.

The island is so big that its owner still hasn't seen the whole thing. And there's a wild part that has never been explored.

The enchanted part is the stuff you can do in the sea at night: from fishing with a lantern to swimming all lit up by the phosphorescence of the sea plants. Ask a grownup to explain to you what phosphorescence means.

The fruits are jackfruit, cashew, hog plum, soursop, bananas. And from the very tall coconut palms lots of coconuts fall, even on top of people's heads if you don't watch out. There are also white and red guavas, and scarlet-colored Brazilian cherries.

The drinking water was canalized with the island's enormous bamboos.

It's such an enchanted island that I'd be afraid to be there all by myself at night in my hammock. On that island is every species of tree, plant, fruit, and flower.

Living on an island forever is sad because we don't want to be separated from our family and friends. But we don't have to live there. It's enough to spend Saturday and Sunday there.

All right, let's leave the island alone, and get back to animals. I have a friend who has a dog who barks so much and so loudly that he almost made me want to bark back.

I get very offended when an animal is scared of me, because I'm brave and protect animals. If any of you are ever scared, I'll take care of you and make you feel better. Since I know what children's fear is like because I was a child myself. To this day I'm still scared of certain things.

Another friend of mine had a dog named Bolinha. She was very normal, more normal than many human people and than many dogs. She was a perfect mother. She took care of her puppies all by herself and licked them instead of bathing them. When my friend came up to her, she'd push her puppies forward with her snout to introduce them. Bolinha taught her kids to run and play.

She was very sensitive and a little nervous. She'd notice people coming from far off. When people were mad, or when she did something wrong, she'd lean against the wall and sit looking out awkwardly.

I don't have any stories to tell about horses, and that's too bad, because horses are animals of great beauty.

Okay, now the time has come to talk about my crime: I killed two little fish. I swear it wasn't on purpose. I swear it wasn't very much my fault. If it was, I'd tell you.

My son went away for a month and asked me to take care of two little red fish in the aquarium.

But that was too long to leave the fishes with me. Not that you can't trust me. But the thing is, I'm very busy, because I also write stories for grownups.

And just like a mother or a maid can forget about a pan on the stove, and when they go check all the food is burned—I was also busy writing a story. And I simply did something like letting the food burn on the stove: I forgot to feed the fish for three days! They who loved to eat so much, poor things.

Besides feeding them, I was supposed to keep changing the aquarium water, so they could swim in clean water.

And it wasn't just any food: it was bought in special stores. The food looked like a horrible little powder, but it must be tasty for fish because they ate it all up.

They must have starved, just like people. But we talk and complain, the dog barks, the cat meows, all animals speak through sounds. But the fish is as mute as a tree and didn't have a voice to complain and call out to me.

And when I went to look, they were still, thin, little, red—and unfortunately already dead of hunger.

Are you all very upset with me because I did that? Then forgive me. I too got very upset with myself for being so distracted. But it was too late to cry over it.

I really would like you to pardon me. From this day forward I'll never get distracted again.

Do you forgive me?

THE END

THE MYSTERY
OF THE THINKING RABBIT
(A DETECTIVE STORY FOR CHILDREN)

This story only works for children who like rabbits. It was written at the request-order of Paulo, when he was small and had yet to discover stronger affections. "The Mystery of the Thinking Rabbit" is also my discreet homage to two rabbits that belonged to Pedro and Paulo, my sons. These rabbits gave us a lot of headaches and lots of delightful surprises. Because the story was written for exclusively domestic use, I left out a lot between the lines for oral explanations. I beg forgiveness from fathers and mothers, uncles and aunts, and grandparents, for the forced contribution they'll have to make. But at least I can guarantee, from personal experience, that the oral part of the story is the best part. It's very nice to talk about rabbits. In any case this "mystery" is more of an intimate conversation than a story. That's why it's much longer than its apparent number of pages. It really only ends when the child discovers other mysteries.

C.L.

Well then, Paulo, you'll never guess what happened with that rabbit.

If you think he started talking, you're wrong. He never said a single word in his whole life. If you think he was any different from other rabbits, you're wrong. To tell you the truth, he was nothing more than a rabbit. The most you can say about him is that he was a very white rabbit.

For all these reasons nobody ever imagined that he might have a few ideas. Pay attention: I didn't say "lots of ideas," I just said "a few." Well then, nobody even thought he could have a few.

The special thing that happened with that rabbit was also special about every rabbit in the world. That was that he'd think those few ideas with his nose. The way he thought his ideas was by moving his nose around really fast. He'd scrunch and unscrunch his nose so much that it was always pink. If you looked at him you'd think he was thinking nonstop. That's not true. It was just his nose that moved fast, not his head. And in order to sniff one single idea, he'd need to scrunch his nose fifteen thousand times.

So anyway. One day Joãozinho's nose—that was the name of this rabbit—one day Joãozinho's nose managed to sniff out something so marvelous that he went nuts. Out of pure joy, his heart beat as fast as if he'd swallowed a bunch of butterflies. Joãozinho said to himself:

"Gee, I'm nothing more than a white rabbit, but I just smelled an idea so good that it seems like something a kid would have thought up!"

And he was thrilled. The idea he'd smelled was as good as the smell of a fresh carrot.

Joãozinho then started working on this idea. And in order to do that he needed to move his nose so much that this time his nose almost turned red. Rabbits have a lot of trouble thinking, because nobody believes that they think. And nobody expects them to think. So much so that the rabbit's nature has already grown used to not thinking. And nowadays all of them are patient and happy. Their nature is to be very satisfied: as long as they're loved, they don't mind being a little dumb.

I'm not sure you know exactly what "a rabbit's nature" means.

A rabbit's nature is the way a rabbit is made. For example: their nature makes more babies than people's nature does. That's why he's a little foolish when it comes to thinking, but he's not foolish at all when it comes to making babies. Whereas a father and a mother slowly have one people-child, rabbits have lots, just like that, without even really trying. And fast, the same way they scrunch and unscrunch their noses.

A rabbit's nature is also the way he figures out which things are good for him, without anyone's having taught him.

A rabbit's nature is also his way of getting on in life.

As I was saying, Joãozinho started working out his idea. This is what the idea was: to escape from the hutch whenever there wasn't any food in the hutch.

You might be disappointed, Paulinho. You might have expected some other kind of idea, you who have so many. But it just so happens that this is a true story. And everyone knows that this is exactly the kind of idea that a rabbit might sniff out. Because his nature is only clever about the things that he needs.

As I was saying, Joãozinho remembered to escape every time he didn't have food in his hutch.

But that was the problem: how could he get out of there?

The hutch had very narrow bars, and Joãozinho, besides being white, was fat. Of course he couldn't get through the bars. The only way to open the hutch was by lifting the covering. And the covering, Paulo, was made of heavy iron, only people could manage to lift it.

For two days Joãozinho scrunched and unscrunched his nose thousands of times in order to see if he could smell the solution. And the idea finally came. This time, Paulo, it was such a good idea that not even children, who have excellent ideas, could guess it.

Here's what the idea was: he figured out how to leave the hutch. And as soon as he thought of it he did it. Suddenly the rabbit's owners saw the rabbit on the sidewalk, cried out, ran after him, called the other kids on the street—and everyone together surrounded Joãozinho and finally managed to catch him.

You're surely expecting me to tell right now how he managed to get out of there.

But that's the mystery: I don't know! And the kids didn't know either. Because, as I told you, the cover was made of heavy iron. Through the bars? Never! Remember that Joãozinho was fat and the bars were close together.

Meanwhile, the kids, who don't have a silly nature, started noticing that the white rabbit would only run off when there was no food in the hutch. So they never again forgot to fill up his plate.

And life, for that white rabbit, started to be very nice. He had no lack of food.

But, Paulo, it just so happens that Joãozinho, having run away a few times, started to like it.

And he started to run away for no reason: just because he felt like it. He had more than enough food. But he really longed to run away. You understand, children don't have to escape because they don't live behind bars.

And of course Joãozinho's heart would beat like a madman's when he'd run away. But that's also because rabbits have very panicky hearts. Just as it's the nature of rabbits to sniff out ideas with their noses.

Eventually Joãozinho's life started to be like this: he'd have a nice meal and then run away, and always with his heart beating. An excellent plan. He'd run away, the kids would grab him, he got food, he was very happy. He was so happy that sometimes his nose would move as fast as if he were smelling the whole world.

Speaking of which, I want to remind you that the world smells much more for rabbits than it does for us. A rabbit's nose is much more useful to him than our noses are for us. Have you ever noticed that a rabbit's nose seems to be always receiving and sending urgent telegrams? That's because he understands things with his nose. That doesn't mean that the rabbit's nature is better than ours. Every nature has its advantages.

I'm going to tell you how the world is made. Like this: when you have a rabbit's nature, the best thing in the world is to be a rabbit, but when you have a person's nature you don't want to live any other way.

Do you think, Paulo, that Joãozinho's owners got mad at him? They sure did. But they got mad the way that a father and mother get mad at their kids: they got mad but they didn't stop liking him. That rabbit, well, you didn't even need to be related to him in order to like him. I'm going to tell you: Joãozinho had a silly face and was handsome. You even wanted to give him a little squeeze. Not too much, because Joãozinho would immediately get scared. Rabbits are like birds: they get scared if you pet them too hard, they're not sure if you're doing it out of love or anger. We have to go slowly to let them get used to it, until they start to trust you.

What do you think Joãozinho would do when he'd run away?

Sometimes I think he ran away to see his girlfriend. His girlfriend was a rabbit very much of the nitpicking and willful type, who would always say to Joãozinho:

"If you don't come see me, I'll forget all about you."

It was a lie, since she loved that rabbit of hers, but that little trick helped her get what she wanted. She didn't say that to Joãozinho because she was wicked, but that's the nature of a girl rabbit. And the way a girl rabbit has of liking someone is a cunning way. Actually almost all girlfriends' natures resemble each other a bit.

I also think that Joãozinho would run away because he kept having more and more babies and he liked to go pet his babies. The babies were all fat, small, and silly, and all of them had a rabbit's nature. Look, Paulinho, if for people it's nice to love a rabbit, just imagine how great it is to love a rabbit when you're its father or mother. Don't even get me started.

Sometimes Joãozinho would run off just to have a look at things, since nobody ever took him for a walk. That's when he really would become a thinking rabbit. He'd go around looking at the things that his nose had figured out, for example, that the earth was round.

There are only two ways to discover that the earth is round: either studying it in books, or being happy. A happy rabbit knows a bunch of things.

Another thing his nose discovered is that clouds move slowly and sometimes create big rabbits in the sky. On his escapades he'd also discover that there are things that are nice to smell but aren't meant to be eaten. And that's when he discovered that liking something is almost as nice as eating it.

Anyway, Paulo—but I'm going to ask you one more time: how did the white rabbit escape through the bars?

Paulinho, this is a real mystery story. It's a story that's so mysterious that to this day I haven't found a single child who could give me a good answer. It's true that not even I, the one who's telling the story, know the answer. What I can promise you is that I'm not lying: Joãozinho really did run off.

You asked me to figure out the mystery of the rabbit's escape. This is how I've tried to figure it out: I sit here scrunching my nose as fast as I can. Just to see if I can manage to think what a rabbit thinks when he scrunches his nose.

But you know very well what just happened. When I scrunch my nose, instead of having an idea, I get this crazy urge to eat carrots. And that, of course, doesn't explain how Joãozinho sniffed out a way to slip through the bars.

If you want to solve the mystery, Paulinho, try scrunching up your nose to see if that works. You might just figure it out, because boys and girls understand more about rabbits than fathers and mothers. When you figure it out, let me know. I'm just going to stop scrunching my nose, because I'm already tired, my dear, of only eating carrots.

THE END

ALMOST TRUE

Once upon a time … Once upon a time: me!

But I bet you don't know who I am. Get ready for a surprise you'll never guess.

You know who I am? I'm a dog named Ulisses and my owner is Clarice. I sit around barking at Clarice and she—who understands what my barks mean—writes down what I tell her. For example, I took a trip to a yard nearby and told Clarice a nicely barked story: soon you'll know all about it: it's the result of something I observed about that house.

First of all I want to take a moment to introduce myself. People say I'm very handsome and clever. It seems I really am handsome. I've got brown guarana-colored fur. But more than anything else it's my eyes that everyone admires: they're golden. My owner didn't want to clip my tail because she thought that goes against nature.

People say: "Ulisses looks at you just like a person." I really like to lie on my back and get my tummy scratched. But I'm only clever when it comes to barking out words.

I'm a little naughty, I don't always obey, I like to do whatever I want, I pee in Clarice's living room.

Besides that, I'm an almost normal dog. Ah, I forgot to say I'm a magic dog: I figure everything out by smelling. That's called following your nose. In the yard where I was staying I sniffed everything: the fig tree, the rooster, the hen, etc.

If you call out: "Ulisses, come here"—I'll come up running and barking because I like children a lot and I only bite when someone hits me. So can I bark out a story that almost seems like make-believe and almost seems true? It's only true in the world of someone who likes to invent things, like you and me. What I'm going to tell you also seems like a human story, even though it takes place in the kingdom where animals talk. They talk in their own way, of course.

But before we get started, I'll ask you in a whisper so that only you can hear:

"Can you hear a little bird singing right this second? If not, pretend you are. It's a little bird that looks as if it's made out of gold, it has a bright red beak and is very happy with life. To help you make up its little tune, I'm going to tell you the way it sings. It sings like this: pirilim-pim-pim, pirilim-pim-pin, pirilim-pim-pim. It's a joyful bird. When I tell you my story I'm going to interrupt it sometimes when I hear the little bird."

So what about the story?

Well, it starts off in the huge yard of a lady named Eniria.

Eniria is a little bit magical herself, but only when she goes into the kitchen. Just think that, with eggs, wheat flour, butter, and chocolate, she manages to make a cake explode that's good enough for a king and queen. Here's a question for you: who's the magical person in the kitchen in your house?

In this yard that I visited and sniffed out, what did I find? There was an enormous tree called a fig tree—and roosters and hens.

Everything was carrying on just fine over there: the rain was feeding the beautiful fig tree, the Sun was giving it life. Eniria would make cakes, not to mention that, besides the corn that the roosters and hens were eating, the ground was full of worms, especially after it rained, such fine soil.

Eniria really liked the big fig tree and the birds. She even had a book that told her how to make hens lay nice sturdy eggs: instead of giving them a little cold water, you'd give them lukewarm water, and plenty of it. As for the fig tree, Eniria would sometimes put fertilized soil on its roots from which it would take food with vitamins.

Out of all the roosters and hens were two birds who were very important because they were smart, nice, and protected their friends. They were like the king and queen of the henhouse. The rooster's name was Evidio. The "E" came from egg, the "vidio" was just because he felt like it. The hen was named Edissea. The "E" was because of egg and the "dissea" was just because she felt like it.

Actually the same thing happened with Eniria: the "E" in egg and the "niria" because that's how she wanted it. Married to Mr. Enofre. Well, you already know that the "E" in Enofre was in honor of the egg— you guessed it: the "nofre" was just messing around. And patati and patatá. Au-au-au!

That's how life went on. Gently, gently.

The men were manning, the women were womaning, the boys and girls were boysandgirlsing, the winds were winding, the rain raining, the hens henning, the roosters roostering, the fig tree figtreeing, the eggs egging. And so forth.

At this point, you must be complaining and asking: where's the story?

Bear with me, the story's going to storify. And right this second. This is how it starts: It was a Sunday, nothing going on, no entertainment, it was a worthless day. I mean, nothing was happening. Everything the same. The Sun singing. The hens were cackling just because they felt like chattering. But the quiet didn't last long. And it was the fault of the fig tree who for some reason had never produced any figs.

(Pirilim-pim-pim, pirilim-pim-pim, pirilim-pim-pim!)

Would you believe that around noon the fig tree, just because she didn't have anything else to do, forced herself to think. The effort was so great that some of her leaves even fell to the ground. And finally she had a thought.

This was the thought:

The life of a rooster and a hen is a true delight.

Evidio crows, the hens lay eggs. But what about me? I, who don't even produce figs?

And patati and patatá.

The fig tree's thought went rotten and turned into envy. It rotted even more and turned into revenge. The fig tree, who didn't produce any fruit and didn't sing, made up her mind to get rich on the others' backs. She wanted to freeload off of Evidio's kids, Edissea and other birds. If at least she could sing she'd forgive them. But she wasn't going to take it a minute longer. (Au, au, au!)

As she went from one thought to the next, all of them filled with rage, the fig tree came up with an unfortunate solution: you'll never guess what she was going to do.

You know what? *That rascally fig tree got in touch with a black cloud that was a witch. And asked:*

"Witch, little witch darling, make all the eggs be mine, even if I can't crow like Evidio! I want to sell those eggs and make a lot of money!"

That's what she said and in her eyes was a little glint of shamelessness.

The bad witch was named Exelia. The "E", etc. etc., you already know all about that. Once she was consulted, she hardly had to think: she was so wicked that

43

she was a cloud who wouldn't even rain. And I'll tell you something else: she wanted to do a favor for the fig tree because she wanted her, at the end, to get in trouble. Sorry, but I'm not going to tell you yet what the end was. Just wait.

Do you want to know what happened after the conversation between the fig tree and Exelia? It was this: at night the fig tree's leaves would turn on as if the Sun were pouring down onto them.

And the hens, thinking it was daytime, would lay eggs. The fig tree had also asked Exelia to make the hens lay their eggs on the ground, next to her roots.

What happened? It just so happened that the hens got scared because they no longer slept and were laying eggs nonstop, all the time.

As for Evidio, he wore himself out: since he thought it was daytime, he went hoarse from all the crowing.

(Pirilim-pim-pim, pirilim-pim-pim, pirilim-pim-pim.)

Meanwhile, the fig tree was gathering eggs like nobody's business and all in order to sell them and become a millionaire. And she didn't pay the hens, not with money, or with worms, or with water. Nothing but slavery.

Edissea, seeing the way things were going, clucked to Evidio:

"We're exhausted, I need to have a serious talk with you."

As she said that, she wearily lay an egg.

(Au, au, au. I'm barking outrageously and Clarice's even looking alarmed.)

Evidio was a rooster who thought a lot, just like Edissea. They were talking at the back of the yard, and patati and patatá, and patati and patatá. They spent two days working out an understanding with bird words.

The result?

The result was really clever.

There was no doubt about it: they were going to fight back against the dictatorial fig tree, insist on their rights, lay eggs for themselves alone, demand food, water, sleep and rest.

You must be thinking that Eniria wasn't taking care of things. Answer: she and Enofre had gone on a trip and didn't know what sort of mischief was happening in the chicken coop.

They'd let a minion take care of everything, but this minion, whose name was Equequê (the "E" for egg, and so on and so forth), this minion was lazy and didn't do anything but eat, sleep, and flirt, without keeping an eye on anything at all.

I should say that by day the fig tree didn't look like anything more than a regular fig tree, so as not to call attention to herself.

When everyone was asleep she turned on all her lights, as she and Exelia had agreed. Edissea and Evidio decided something that you're going to find out about right this second. They whispered the decision to the other birds in a patati and patatá.

And when the dangerous night arrived and the fig tree bewitched with its twinkles of lights—well, all of the hens, headed up by their president and first lady, which is to say, by Evidio and Edissea, made an effort to fly and perched on the branches of the fig tree. And from up there they started laying eggs.

Did you think that was just silliness on their part?

Well, au, au, au, that's where you're wrong. What was going on?

What was going on is that the eggs were landing on the ground, every last one of them would break, and there were shells here, yolks there, whites over there, all rotting on the ground. Was it a shame to sacrifice so many eggs? Sure, but sometimes you have to make a sacrifice.

The fig tree was horrified by all that waste. It was a huge loss. And she didn't even like omelettes. And the eggs kept on falling. Every egg that fell made this noise when it hit the ground: pló-quiti, pló-quiti, pló-quiti.

At the same time, Evidio started to crow:

"We demand the freedom to sing only during the day!"

The hens clucked at the same time:

"We demand to lay eggs only when we feel like it, and we want to keep our own eggs! They're our kids!"

The ruckus was practically deafening the fig tree. She really wanted to check with the witch about what to do. But Exelia was busy with something else, something that was wicked too.

The fig tree was going nuts and begged for special help, like going to the doctor (except doctors are good), and the sorceress Exelia, darker and darker, agreed to give her an answer.

As I, Ulisses the dog, said at the beginning, Exelia was so wicked that she wanted bad things to happen to the fig tree too, the one who up till now had been her partner in evil. And she said:

"Consider yourself lucky! since I could punish you by ordering up a storm at night and making a bolt of lightning strike you right on your crown and split your proud trunk in two!"

The hens and roosters were free, finally! And they went to sleep, since they needed to after so many nights of insomnia.

The fig tree was stunned: she didn't know until then not to be friends with bad folks.

Then, very humiliated, she saw her lights go out.

At dawn, Evidio sang more beautifully than ever before. And the hens stretched out happily.

Everyone was so pleased that Evidio and Edissea decided to throw a party. And, to please the birds, they bought a thousand lollipops.

It just so happened, however, that they didn't realized that a lollipop is something to suck or lick and they started biting them: crack, crack, crack with their teeth. What happened? what happened was that all their teeth broke. That's why birds don't have teeth. At least that's what I think, au, au, au.

(Pirilim-pim-pim, pirilim-pim-pim, pirilim-pim-pim.)

That's when Eniria and Enofre came back from their trip. And they found the poultry so happy and they enjoyed seeing them. But they noticed that they no longer had any teeth. That's when Eniria said to Enofre:

"Let's have them visit other places because they might just find some new food that doesn't need to be chewed!"

Said and done. And soon they let Evidio and Edissea take the whole crew out for a walk. The countryside was gorgeous: nice fresh green grass where the birds could rub their beaks. Delicious.

But then they got hungry. And where was there anything to eat? Well then. Evidio and Edissea remembered a witch, one of the good ones, named Exalá—the "E" for egg, "xalá" just to show off. She was magic and granted their wish. She led them into the woods and showed them a jabuticaba tree. You know what a jabuticaba is? It's a round black fruit that only exists in Brazil.

Evidio and Edissea were pleased because they knew that Exalá always did whatever she promised. So they asked for more.

"Exalá darling, is there any way you could make the black cloud, Exelia, stop being so evil?"

Exalá smiled and said:

"Well now: she won't be dangerous any more and in just a few hours she's going to rain. And she'll rain on top of the fig tree. But now I'm going to tell you something: the jabuticaba is a fruit you can eat, even if you don't have teeth."

A little bit scared, the birds took the jabuticabas with their beaks. And with just their beaks the little fruits burst. The noise sounded like this: plique-ti, plique-ti, plique-ti.

They just loved the jabuticaba. Even though it had a little bitter aftertaste. As you know, the jabuticaba has a pit that's sweet and that gets a little bitter after you suck on it.

They grow on the jabuticaba tree, both on the branches and on the trunk, filling it up with thousands of jabuticabas. These, when they're nice and ripe and round, fall to the ground. When you step on them they make a noise like this: plóqui-ti-ti, plóqui-ti-ti, plóqui-ti-ti.

The roosters and hens had a great time stepping on them: the sound was a delight, it gave you a nice little rush. But they still hadn't figured out that the fruit was meant to be eaten.

Meanwhile, Edissea said to Evidio:

"Now that we're free and happy, should we forgive the fig tree who's so sad? I think she regrets it. Should we ask Exalá to take care of her?"

"Done," Evidio answered.

They looked up to the sky and saw Exalá.

She was beautiful in the bright blue sky: white and golden and bright from the Sun that was shining on her. She heard the request for forgiveness and said:

"Fine, I'll forgive the fig tree. And I'll even go further: I'm going to make her have babies, I mean, figs."

But something happened: the birds still had the pits of the jabuticabas in their mouths and didn't know what to do.

So they asked Edissea and Evidio:

"Do we swallow the pit or not?"

Evidio and Edissea were astounded: they didn't know what to say. They thought about asking Exalá for help but they thought they'd already asked her enough and needed to figure it out by themselves.

(Pirilim-pim-pim, pirilim-pim-pim, pirilim-pim-pim.)

I, who am a dog, don't know what to tell the birds.

"Do you swallow the pit or not?"

You, kid, ask a grownup.

Meanwhile, I'll say:

"Au, au, au!"
And Clarice understands what I mean:
"See you later, kid! Do you swallow the pit or not?"
That is the question.

THE END

LAURA'S INTIMATE LIFE

To Nicole Algranti
To Andréa Azulay
To Alexandre Dines
To Fátima Froldi

To Fabiana Colasanti de Sant'Anna

Let me start off right away explaining what "intimate life" means. It's this: intimate life means we shouldn't tell everyone what goes on at our house. They're things you don't tell just anyone.

So I'm going to tell you about Laura's intimate life.

Now guess who Laura is.

I'll give you a kiss on the forehead if you guess it. And I doubt you'll get it right! Three guesses.

See how hard it is?

Because Laura is a hen.

And a really simple hen at that.

I ask you to do me a favor and like Laura straightaway because she's the nicest hen I've ever seen. She lives in Miss Luísa's yard with the other birds. She's married to a rooster named Luís. Luís likes Laura a lot, though he sometimes fights with her. But they're little fights about nothing.

I think I'm going to have to tell you the truth. The truth is that Laura has the ugliest neck I've ever seen in the whole world. But you don't care, do you? Because what really matters is being pretty on the inside. Are you beautiful on the inside? I bet you are. How do I know? Because I'm guessing who you are.

Another truth: Laura's pretty dumb. Some people think she's *really* dumb, but that's going too far: anyone who knows Laura well knows that she has her little thoughts and little feelings. Not many, but she's definitely got them. Just knowing she's not completely dumb makes her all chatty and giddy. She thinks that she thinks. But for the most part she's not thinking about anything at all.

Luís struts around all day long in the yard among the hens, his chest puffed up with vanity. That's because he thinks that, since he knows how to sing at dawn, he's in charge of the Moon and the Sun.

Laura won't let almost anyone pet her. Because she's simply terrified of people. If anyone gets close to her, unless it's to give her corn, she runs off in a great clatter, clucking like a madwoman. This is what she clucks: don't kill me! don't kill me!

But nobody intends to kill her because she's the hen who lays the most eggs in the whole coop and even in the whole neighborhood.

Laura's always in something of a rush. What's the rush, dear Laura? Since she's got nothing to do. This rushing around is one of Laura's silly habits. But she's modest: all she needs is to cluck out an endless chat with the other hens. The others are a lot like her: also part brown and part reddish. Only one hen is different from them: a leghorn with black-and-white coloring all over. But they don't look down on the leghorn just because she belongs to another race. They even seem to know that for God there's none of this silliness about one race being better than another.

I know you've never seen Laura. But if you've ever seen a hen who's part reddish, part yellowish, and with a really ugly neck, then it's as if you were looking at Laura.

There will always be a hen like Laura and there will always be a child like you. Isn't that great? That way we never feel lonely.

It's too bad that Laura doesn't like a single person. She almost never has feelings, as I said. Most of the time she has the same feelings that a shoe box must have.

Why might it be that Laura spends the whole day pecking at the ground and looking for food? It can't be because she's really that hungry, since Miss Luísa, the cook, gives her plenty of corn. I'm going to tell one of Laura's secrets: she eats out of pure obsession. She'll eat the nastiest things! But she's not as dumb as she seems. For example: she doesn't eat pieces of glass. Pretty clever, right?

One day she felt that she was going to be a mother

again. She quickly clucked the news to Luís. Luís looked like he was going to explode out of so much vanity about being a father again. I'm well aware that every egg is born. But this one was going to be a beauty. It was a very special egg.

Until one night Laura felt that the egg was ready to be born. How did she feel it? I'm sorry, I don't know, because I've never been a hen in my whole life. She was even asleep and woke up feeling the egg being born from her.

Long live my child! That's what Luís sang. Even though it was midnight, the news was like the Sun shining. In the henhouse that lovely white egg was shining. Laura, all pleased with herself, rubbed her feathers with her beak in order to smooth herself out, the same way people comb their hair. Because she's very vain and very much enjoys looking good.

After she'd tidied up she saw she was ready to sit on top of the egg and warm it up until the chick was born. Everything was so nice that I can't even tell you.

Her girlfriends came to visit, all of them clucking and bringing worms as gifts, since she couldn't get off the egg.

Miss Luísa also visited her. As a present from Miss Luísa, Laura got a new yellow dish for her corn.

When the chick was ready, too big to fit inside his shell, he himself broke the shell from the inside out with his beak.

After he came out all in one piece from the eggshell, that ugly skinny little thing appeared.

But the next day he became the yellowest and cutest chick in the world, and started running after his mother. Laura gathered worms and stuck the worms into the chick's open beak. Until he started growing and became a chicken and then he himself started looking for food to eat. He'd already caught Laura's own obsession: he'd eat without stopping. Laura was as satisfied as a queen.

This chicken's name is Hermany.

One fine night ... It wasn't fine at all! Because it was terrible. A chicken thief tried to steal Laura in the darkness from the yard. But Laura made such a tremendous noise that she woke up all the hens and they started to crow. And the rooster started to shriek.

Miss Luísa turned on all the lights in the house, turned on the lights in the yard and the thief got so scared that he ran off. They say he's running to this day.

Another bad thing for Laura was that Miss Luísa loaned her to a neighboring yard. Because she knew how to lay lots of eggs and they asked to borrow her for a while.

That's how Laura ended up surrounded by hens she didn't know and without Luís.

Afterward things got better because she started to make friends with the hens and laid lots and lots of eggs.

Then she went back to her real yard. Luís was very

pleased. This rooster, as I've already said, was very vain. He was proud to be married to Laura, proud of singing so loudly, hoarsely, and raucously, as soon as the Sun gave any sign of wanting to rise. He was the first rooster in the whole area to crow.

When I was as big as you are now, I'd spend hours and hours looking at the hens. I don't know why. I know hens so well that I could tell you about them forever and ever.

I'm going to tell something a little bit gross. Here goes: do you know that a hen has a slightly nasty smell? It's like the smell of a basket of dirty laundry or when you don't bathe every day. It's not a clean smell at all. So under their wings there's that stench. But it doesn't matter. Every single thing has its smell, right? Do you smell nice? Dogs are the ones who spend all their time smelling stuff. What I'd like to know is who taught the rooster to sing at dawn. There are people who use their singing like an alarm clock in order to wake up.

I'd so much like for Laura to be able to talk. She'd say so many funny silly things that it would be a sight to see. She'd say for example: "do you know that a red thing is red?" and you'd answer: of course it is, if you say so.

Maybe she'd be able to explain the taste of a worm. But it's not easy to explain the taste of something in your mouth. For example: try to explain what chocolate tastes like. See how hard it is? It just tastes like chocolate.

Did you know that God likes hens? And do you know how I know He likes them? Here's why: if He didn't like hens, He simply wouldn't make hens in the world. God likes you too because otherwise He wouldn't have made you. But why does he make rats? I don't know.

Laura doesn't kiss anybody. I think she might give a few awkward little pecks to Hermany. In any case I never saw anyone more awkward than this hen. Everything she does is a bit off. Except eating. And, of course, she makes an egg just right.

There's a way to eat hens called "hen in black sauce." Have you ever eaten it? The sauce is made with the hen's blood. But you can't buy a dead hen: she has to be alive and killed at home in order to be able to use the blood. And I don't do that. I don't kill hens. But it's tasty. You eat it with nicely cooked white rice.

There's also a way of eating hens called chicken supreme. I just got hungry. I know where you can eat hens this way. But I won't tell you because it'll sound like advertising. Also, for the same reason, I can't say what kind of soda is good to drink with this kind of hen. Guess! It starts with a C.

It's odd to like living hens but also at the same time to like to eat hen in black sauce. It's because humans are a pretty weird type of person.

I'd just like to know one thing: how long have hens been on the Earth? I'm asking you because I don't know.

Now I'm going to tell you something a little sad.

The cook said to Miss Luísa while pointing to Laura:

"That hen isn't laying many eggs and is getting old. Before she gets sick or dies of old age we could cook her in black sauce."

"I won't ever kill that one," Miss Luísa said.

Laura heard it all and was afraid. If she could have thought about it, she would have thought this: it's much better to die being useful and tasty for people who always treated me well, these people for example who never killed me once. (This hen is so dumb that she doesn't know that you only die once, she thinks we die once a day.)

Besides that Laura might be feeling, if she were feeling anything, that Miss Luísa would never eat her. She really liked living. So she stuck her beak into the mud, splattered it all over herself and ruffled her feathers. You can tell she's really not that dumb after all: she knew that the others only really recognized her because she was the cleanest and the tidiest of the whole chicken coop. When the cook showed up Laura got scared, but reassured herself as to Miss Luísa's goodness and love. The cook grabbed a hen named Zeferina, half-reddish and half-brown, who looked a lot like Laura.

And at dinnertime, when everyone was sitting around the table, Zeferina, Laura's fourth cousin, showed up on a big silver platter, already cut into pieces, some nicely browned. Miss Luísa's son and daughter, Lucinha and Carlinhos, ate, though with regret, Zeferina with well-cooked white rice and poured black sauce over the whole thing.

Now I'm going to tell you something really cool. First of all I need to tell you that Laura was a quite advanced hen. So much so that an inhabitant of Jupiter—a guy who only had one eye in his forehead and was the same size as a hen—this inhabitant of Jupiter came down one night into Miss Luísa's yard, while all the hens were asleep.

The dwarf-inhabitant was named Xext and he went straightaway to wake up Laura. Laura wasn't even startled. This is what she said:

"Hi, fellow. What's your name?"

"Xext," he answered.

"Whatever you say," said Laura.

And she asked: "Do you want me to tell Luís to sing out that you've arrived?"

"No," said Xext, "because he'd wake everyone up. And it wouldn't be worth it because people don't believe in me, they think I'm a ghost."

"Why did you choose me to introduce yourself to?"

"Because you're not square."

Xext is pronounced Equzequte. It's hard, I know. It would be easier if he were called José or Zequinha.

Xext asked Laura what humans were like on the inside.

"Ah," Laura squawked, "humans are really compli-cated on the inside. They even feel like they have to lie, imagine that."

"Ask me to do something and I'll make it happen," said Xext.

"Ah," said Laura, "if it's my destiny to be eaten, I want to be eaten by Pelé!"

"But you're never going to be eaten and nobody's going to kill you. Because I won't let them. And now I've got to go, my mother's waiting for me. Her name is Xexta."

"See you," said Laura.

"See you later," Xext answered and disappeared.

How nice to be protected by an inhabitant of Jupiter, Laura thought and went back to sleep. But waking up in the middle of the night wore Laura out, and the next day the cook said to Miss Luísa:

"Laura's got a yesterday face."

"A yesterday face" means she looks like she didn't sleep well.

Here's where the story of Laura and her adventures ends. At the end of the day, Laura has a very nice little life.

If you know any stories about hens, I want to hear them. Or make up a really good one and tell me.

Laura's nice and alive.

THE END